Star Friends
HIDDEN CHARM

To my Sunday team, who have huge imaginations:
Lucia, Imogen, Edward, Mia, Elissa, Harriet, and Spike.
P.S. Why always GNOMES?!—L.C.

tiger tales

5 River Road, Suite 128, Wilton, CT 06897
Published in the United States 2022
Originally published in Great Britain 2019
by the Little Tiger Group
Text copyright © 2019 Linda Chapman
Illustrations copyright © 2019 Lucy Fleming and Mike Love
ISBN-13: 978-1-6643-4030-5
ISBN-10: 1-6643-4030-0
Printed in China
STP/1800/0453/0322
2 4 6 8 10 9 7 5 3 1

www.tigertalesbooks.com

Star Friends
Hidden Charm

BY LINDA CHAPMAN
ILLUSTRATED BY LUCY FLEMING

tiger tales

Contents

1
In The Star World

The trees in the forest glittered with stardust.
In a secret clearing, a wolf with silver-tipped
fur gazed into a pool of mirror-like water.
A picture on the surface of the pool showed
four girls sitting in a circle, each with a young
animal beside her. The wolf's gaze lingered
longest on the girl with shoulder-length dark-
blond hair. The fox cuddled up to her had
large pricked ears, a white tip on his bushy
tail, and a mischievous look in his indigo eyes.

The silver wolf's ears twitched as a snowy

owl came flying through the black sky with a soft hoot. He landed on a tree branch beside her, his feathers shining. A stag with magnificent antlers stepped silently from the shadows, and a badger came shuffling out of the bushes.

"Greetings," said the wolf.

The stag looked at the picture in the forest pool. "Are you watching our friends in Westport again?"

The wolf nodded. She and the other elder Star Animals used the magic pool to watch over the young Star Animals who had traveled to the human world. Each animal had to find a child to be his or her Star Friend. The animal taught that child how to use the magic current that flowed between the Star World and the human world to do magic and help people.

"Mia and her friends have learned a lot about magic since they became Star Friends," said Hunter the owl.

"But they have not yet solved the latest

mystery," the badger said, watching as the red squirrel scurried up the arm of the girl he was sitting by and tickled her with his tiny paws. "They do not know who conjured the Shades that caused so much trouble last week."

Shades were evil spirits who lived in the shadows. They could be conjured by people using dark magic and trapped inside everyday objects. They brought chaos and misery wherever they went, and the Star Friends had to work with their Star Animals to send them back to the shadows.

"It is an unusual case this time," said Hunter thoughtfully.

"It is, but anyone using dark magic must be stopped—no matter their reasons," said the stag.

"Let us see if the Star Friends in Westport can find out the identity of the person before more trouble comes," said the badger.

The animals nodded and settled down to watch.

2
An Unsolved Mystery

"This is so annoying!" Violet looked at her friends in frustration as they sat in the clearing. "I hate that there's a mystery we haven't solved!"

Her Star Animal, Sorrel—a wildcat— swished her long tabby tail. "It's been more than a week since we discovered that Shades were causing the strange events happening in town, and we still haven't found out who conjured them from the shadows."

"I know, but we've all been busy," Lexi pointed out, cuddling Juniper, her red squirrel.

"We all had family things going on during the school break, so we couldn't meet up then."

"And after that I was on vacation," added Sita, her arm around Willow, her fallow deer.

"I was away for a few days, too," said Mia, pushing her blond bangs out of her eyes and kissing Bracken, her fox, on the nose.

"Well, now that we're all back together, we can figure out what's going on," said Violet. "We have a few days until school starts again. Hopefully that will be enough time to solve the mystery and stop whoever it is from conjuring Shades again."

Mia rubbed Bracken's russet fur. Violet was right: They had to figure out what was going on. The week before last, they had found some horrible Shades trapped in dolls in the house of an older couple, Ana and Mike Jefferson, who lived in town. The Shades had been trying to make Mr. Jefferson's heart's desire—for Westport to win the contest for Prettiest Small

Town—come true. The town had won the
title, but the Shades' actions had upset everyone,
including Mr. Jefferson. They'd stolen play
equipment from people's yards, dug up flower
beds, cut down ivy from houses, and locked up
pet cats and the ducks from the pond. Luckily,
Mia and the others had tracked the Shades
down and sent them back to the shadows.

"Should I see if the magic can give me
any clues that might help?" Mia said, pulling
a small mirror from her pocket. The others
nodded eagerly.

They had all learned to use the magic current to do different types of magic. Mia could look into a shining surface and see things that were happening in other places. She could also look into the past and the future, and ask the magic to show her things that might help the Star Friends. Sometimes she had magic dreams that gave her important information.

Lexi could use the magic current to become very agile, and she had recently developed the ability to sense when danger was approaching. Sita could heal wounds and command people to do whatever she wanted, although she didn't like making people obey her, so she only used that power in emergencies. Violet could travel to different places, using shadows, and she could cast glamours—disguising objects or people. She was also a Spirit Speaker, which meant that she could send Shades back to the shadows.

Mia took a deep breath. *Don't think about anything else; just think about the magic,* she told herself. She focused on the mirror and felt herself connect with the current. It always felt as if a door had opened in her mind, allowing the magic current to surge into her, tingling through her veins.

"Show me anything that will help us figure out who put the Shades in the dolls," she breathed into the mirror.

Her own reflection faded, and she saw a picture of the main street that led into town—there was a row of houses and the Copper Kettle café. She had seen the same image when they were trying to find the Heart's Desire Shades. The image faded to be replaced by another picture she had seen previously—a small, rectangular black object. Mia still couldn't tell what it was…. Maybe a TV remote? Before she could get a good look, that image faded, too, and became a woman looking into a mirror with lights all around it. The woman in the mirror had red hair. Whenever she had seen the image before, Mia had always felt that there was something odd about it, but she could never figure out what. Before she could put her finger on it, a new image appeared—a necklace made of multicolored beads with a large silver pendant in the shape of an M. The pictures faded, and Mia found herself staring at her own reflection again.

"Well?" Bracken asked as Mia looked up at them.

She reported what she'd seen. "I just keep seeing the same things—the main street by the Copper Kettle, a TV remote, and a woman looking in a mirror. Although there was one new picture—a necklace. I don't know what they all mean."

The others swapped uncertain looks.

"You used to also see the Jeffersons' house next to the ivy-covered house," said Violet.

"I'm not seeing that anymore," said Mia. "But I guess that's because we got rid of the Shades who were in Mrs. Jefferson's dolls."

"Well, this is no good," said Sorrel, getting up and stalking around. "Sitting here like day-old kittens won't solve the mystery— we need a plan of action. If the magic clues aren't helping, then I suggest we start by trying to find out if the people who own the dolls have any enemies."

"That makes sense," said Lexi. "After all, only someone who dislikes the Jeffersons would have put Shades in their dolls."

"But no one dislikes them," said Sita.

Mrs. Jefferson was a school principal, and Mr. Jefferson was chair of the school's Parent Teacher Student Association and did a lot of fundraising. They were very popular in town.

"There *has* to be someone who doesn't like them for the Shades to have been put in Mrs. Jefferson's dolls. Let's go and see if they're home," said Mia, getting to her feet.

"Yes, then come back and tell us what they said!" Bracken said eagerly, jumping up, too, and almost knocking Sorrel over.

Sorrel's tail puffed up. "Watch it, fox!"

"You shouldn't be so slow, cat!" Bracken pounced on her tail and tweaked the hairs at the end of it with his teeth. "Got you!"

Sorrel swiped at him furiously with a paw. Bracken darted back, hiding behind Mia's legs. "Slowpoke!" he teased.

Sorrel hissed again.

"Just ignore him, Sorrel," Violet said, rubbing the wildcat's head. Bracken often

teased Sorrel, and she always got angry.
Sorrel rubbed her forehead against Violet's
hand, and her fur flattened as she calmed
down. She was sharp-tongued, but she adored
Violet.

"Time to get going," Juniper said to the
girls, waving at them with his paw. "Call for
us and tell us what you've found out as soon
as you can."

"We will," they promised.

The animals vanished and would reappear
as soon as the girls called their names.

"Off to the Jeffersons' house," said Lexi,
turning a cartwheel on the soft grass.

Mia grinned. "To try to solve the mystery
at last!"

3
An Exciting Visit

The girls headed down the path that led out of the clearing, pushing the overgrown brambles out of the way. The path came out on a quiet, stony track opposite a pretty house where Mia's Grandma Anne used to live before she died. Mia had recently found out that her grandma had been a Star Friend, too, and that her Star Animal had been a beautiful silver wolf.

She really wished her grandma was still alive. It would have been amazing to do magic together and talk about the Star World.

And not just that: more and more Mia felt that she would like to talk to her grandma about all of the other things that were happening in her normal, non-magic life—the fifth-grade exams that were coming up, her first long school trip when she would be away from home for four nights, and starting middle school in September.

There were so many new things happening! It was a little scary. But, she reminded herself, becoming a Star Friend had been a new thing once. Her life had changed hugely when she'd met Bracken, and she would never wish to go back to how it had been before. Doing magic and being his Star Friend was amazing!

Mia and the others turned left on the path and headed up the hill toward town. At the top of the path, beside the main road, there was a row of stone houses where Violet lived with her mom and dad.

"Wait a sec," Violet said. "Let me just ask Mom something."

She dashed inside and came out a few minutes later, grinning and waving a ten-dollar bill. "Mom gave me this so we can get ice cream from the Copper Kettle on our way!"

"Yum!" said Mia. The Copper Kettle had the best homemade ice cream ever!

They crossed over the busy main street at the top of the road. The Copper Kettle was on the other side. It had a large bay window and was very cozy inside, with an old-fashioned glass counter filled with cakes and pastries, and two large rooms with round tables and mismatched chairs. In the winter, a fire always burned in the grate, but now that it was spring, there was a large bunch of flowers in the fireplace, arranged inside an old copper kettle. Dried flowers and antique pans hung from the ceiling, and there were shelves on the walls with displays of Victorian baby dolls

and old-fashioned teddy bears. A hat rack
stood beside the cash register, and there was
a wooden newspaper rack on the wall by the
door. Mary, who ran the café, was an older
lady with short brown hair, and she lived in an
apartment above the café.

When the girls opened the door, they saw
that Mary was sitting behind the counter,
reading a magazine. There were no customers
at the tables. "Hello, girls," she said. "What
can I get you?"

"Ice cream, please," said Violet.

They all chose what they would like—vanilla for Mia, chocolate for Lexi, mint chocolate chip for Violet, and strawberry for Sita.

"It's very quiet today," Violet said, looking around at the empty café.

Mary sighed. "I've never known business to be so bad at this time of year. People used to stop here as they traveled down the coast, but now they seem to be driving on and heading for the new marina instead."

A few months ago, a marina had opened farther along the coastal road—there was a water park, a hotel, and a café.

"You should put a big sign up advertising your ice cream so people stop here instead," said Mia, licking her cone. "It's the best ice cream in the world!"

"It's my grandma's special recipe," said Mary, "made with just a touch of Cornish magic!"

But although she smiled, Mia could see the worry in her face. "I do hope things improve. If they don't, I may have to shut the café. I can't keep it going with no customers. I was hoping that winning Prettiest Small Town might help, but it hasn't."

"You can't close down," Lexi said in dismay. "We love coming here."

Mary smiled at them. "Well, if you think of any clever plans to drum up some more business, then let me know."

"We will," Mia promised.

They said good-bye and left.

"I wish there was a way we could help Mary using magic," said Violet.

"So do I," said Mia. "But I don't see how."

"I guess there are some things even magic can't help with," said Sita. "Like starting middle school and state tests."

"And having a mom who makes you practice for them all the time," groaned Lexi.

She glanced at Sita. "Though maybe you could command her not to?"

"No!" said Sita firmly. She sighed. "I hope the exams are going to be okay. I'm really worried about them."

"They'll be easy. Don't stress," said Violet airily. She was very smart.

Mia glanced at Sita. She didn't look convinced.

As they passed the duck pond on the village green, they discussed their plan. The girls decided that it might seem odd if they all showed up at the Jeffersons' house, and that it would be better if Mia went by herself.

"I'll ask if Lucia's home," said Mia. Lucia was the Jeffersons' young granddaughter. She was in kindergarten at school, and Mia was her fifth-grade buddy. Mia left the others and went on alone to the Jeffersons' house. Mr. Jefferson was in the yard, doing some weeding, and Mrs. Jefferson was talking to him.

"Hi, Mia," said Mrs. Jefferson as Mia opened the gate. She was in her late fifties with dark hair. She'd grown up in Portugal but had lived in Westport for many years. She and Mr. Jefferson were moving to live in Portugal after the summer. He was a little older than Mrs. Jefferson and was very tall and slim with a broad smile.

"Hi!" Mia said. "Is Lucia with you today?"

Mrs. Jefferson nodded. "She is, and I'm sure she'd love to see you. Lucia! Mia's here!" she called, standing by the front door. "Come on in," she said, beckoning Mia inside.

Lucia ran down the stairs, her pigtails bobbing. "Mia!" she squealed. "Come and see the cookies I made with Nana!"

She grabbed Mia by the hand and pulled her into the kitchen. As they passed the dining room, Mia caught sight of Mrs. Jefferson's collection of old-fashioned foreign dolls on the window ledge. A shiver ran down her spine. Last time she'd been in the house, the dolls had been possessed by Shades, and they had attacked her and the others. They were just normal dolls again now, but Mia still found them creepy.

In the kitchen, a batch of cookies was cooling on the rack. "Would you two like to frost them with me?" Mrs. Jefferson said, washing her hands.

"Yes, please," said Mia. It would be a great chance to get her talking.

They settled down at the table with spoons

and a bowl full of frosting. As they began to frost the cookies, Mia tried to figure out how she was going to ask Mrs. Jefferson if there was anyone who might not like her and her husband. It was a strange question to just come out with!

"Can I have a cookie, Nana?" Lucia said.

"Sure," said Mrs. Jefferson with a smile. "Mia, do you want one?"

"Thanks, but I'm full at the moment," said Mia. "I just had an ice cream."

"From the Copper Kettle? Were there many people in there?" Mrs. Jefferson asked.

"No, it was really quiet," said Mia.

"Poor Mary," sighed Mrs. Jefferson. "It's such a shame that the new marina went ahead. It's been bad for her business. Mike tried to oppose it when it was at the planning stage—he knew it would affect the shops here in Westport—but it went ahead anyway. Desmond Hannigan has disliked Mike ever since."

Mia's ears pricked up at the mention of someone who didn't like Mr. Jefferson. "Desmond Hannigan? Who's he?"

"The owner of the marina," said Mrs. Jefferson. She smiled. "Still, if in 60 years you've only made one enemy in life, then that's a life lived well as far as I'm concerned."

Mia stored the information in her head. So Mr. Jefferson only had one enemy, and it was this Desmond Hannigan. Maybe he was responsible for putting the Shades in the dolls….

"The cookies are yummy, Nana," said Lucia, licking her fingers.

Mrs. Jefferson smiled. "It's a recipe from Portugal."

"You made them for the PTSA psychic evening that Mr. Jefferson organized, didn't you?" Mia remembered. "When that lady, Mystic Maureen, came and told people's fortunes?"

Mrs. Jefferson nodded. "Yes, that was a great evening. It was actually Mary at the Copper Kettle who suggested it. She gave one of Mystic Maureen's business cards to Mike, and it turned out to be a real fundraiser. Look." She took a photo off the fridge and handed it to Mia.

Mia glanced at the photo. It showed Mystic Maureen and some of the parents with Mr. Jefferson. Mia remembered the fortune-teller well. She had shoulder-length red hair and was wearing a colorful dress and an unusual scarf.

She was about to hand the photo back when something caught her eye. Around Mystic Maureen's neck there was a necklace with a large pendant in the shape of an M.

Mia froze. It was the same necklace the magic had shown her! She studied the photo closely, remembering that the magic had also shown her someone sitting at a mirror. Excitement swirled inside her as she realized that the person she had seen in the mirror looked like Mystic Maureen!

Could Mystic Maureen have had something to do with the Shades in Mrs. Jefferson's dolls? The timing fit—the Shades had started to do things in town just after the fortune-telling evening. And, now that Mia thought about it, Mystic Maureen had seemed really interested in the dolls. She'd told Mrs. Jefferson she collected dolls herself and had taken photos of the ones Mrs. Jefferson had. Thinking back, it was suspicious.

"Are you okay, Mia?" Mrs. Jefferson asked, and Mia realized she was still staring at the photo.

"Yes, I'm fine," she said, handing it back. But inside she was more than fine; she was jumping up and down with excitement. She couldn't wait to tell the others what she had found out!

4
A Clue!

Mia was almost bursting with her news by the time she left the Jeffersons' house. The others were waiting on the bench by the duck pond.

"You've discovered something, haven't you?" Sita asked, seeing her excited face.

"Yes! Listen to this!" Mia pulled them into a huddle and told them everything. "I think the magic was trying to tell me that it was Mystic Maureen who put the Shades in the dolls," she finished. "I'm sure it was her looking in the mirror, and it showed me her necklace, too."

"What about the other things it showed you—the main street, and the thing that looked like a remote control?" said Lexi. "How do they fit in?"

Mia shrugged impatiently. "I don't know, but the important thing is that we find Mystic Maureen!"

"So how do we do that?" said Violet.

Mia remembered something. "Mrs. Jefferson told me that Mary gave Mr. Jefferson one of Mystic Maureen's business cards. There must be some at the Copper Kettle. If we can get one, it should have a phone number or address on it."

"The Copper Kettle!" Violet exclaimed suddenly. "You said the part of the street that the magic showed you had the Copper Kettle on it, and Mystic Maureen's cards are in the Copper Kettle. Maybe the magic was trying to tell you that the Copper Kettle is important and we should go there."

"Yes! Let's go now!" said Mia.

"This is so good! We finally have a suspect!" said Violet as they set off. "I can't wait to tell Sorrel!"

"I wonder why Mystic Maureen would put Shades in the dolls," said Lexi.

"I have no idea," said Mia. "She seemed perfectly friendly with the Jeffersons that evening, and Mrs. Jefferson just told me that Mr. Jefferson has no enemies except for a man named Desmond Hannigan, who owns the new marina."

"We definitely need to question her and find out what's going on!" said Sita.

When the girls arrived at the Copper Kettle, there was no one inside.

"With you in a minute!" Mary's voice called from the kitchen.

Violet went to the front desk. Beside the

cash register was a selection of flyers and local business cards. "I can't see any cards for Mystic Maureen," she said.

Mia joined her. There were business cards for florists, pet sitters, plumbers, and babysitters, but none for Mystic Maureen.

"Hello, girls. Back again already?" They looked up as Mary came from the kitchen area, dusting flour off her hands onto her apron. "I was just trying out a new recipe for cakes, another one from my grandma's recipe book. What can I get you? More ice cream?"

Mia smiled. "No, thank you. Actually, we just came in to see if you have any business cards for Mystic Maureen, the fortune-teller?"

"Mystic Maureen?" Mary looked a bit surprised. "Goodness. Why do you want one of her cards?"

"She did a fundraising evening for the PTSA," Mia said. "My mom was there and asked me to pick up one of her cards," she fibbed.

"I think there were a few here," Mary began as she looked around on the counter, "but I'm afraid they're all gone now."

"Oh," said Violet in disappointment.

"I don't suppose you know anything about her?" said Lexi hopefully. "Like where she lives?"

"Not really." Mary cleared her throat. "She's only been in a few times. I seem to remember she said she was based at the new marina, but I can't be sure. Now … um … if that's all, I'd really better get back to my baking!" She hurried to the kitchen.

The girls left the café and headed for the clearing to tell the animals what they'd found out.

"It's annoying that there weren't any of Mystic Maureen's cards left," Violet said in a low voice. "What are we going to do now?"

"We could look on the internet," Lexi
suggested. "She may have a website." She
pulled out her phone. "I'll put in Mystic
Maureen, fortune-teller." There was a pause,
and then her forehead furrowed. "Nothing."

"Maybe you're spelling her name wrong,"
said Sita.

Lexi tried again with different spellings.
"No, still nothing," she said after a few more
attempts. "No mention of her at all."

"Then I guess she doesn't have a website,"
suggested Sita.

"Mary said she thinks she's based at the
marina. How about we go there tomorrow
morning and see if we can find her?" said
Violet. "It's too late now. Mia's mom will start
to wonder where we are if we don't go back
soon."

They were having a sleepover at Mia's
that night.

"We could go to the marina after breakfast," Mia suggested.

"We'll need someone to give us a ride," Lexi pointed out.

"We don't need anyone to drive us," Violet said. She looked at their confused faces and grinned. "I can shadow-travel us all there!"

As the girls walked back to Mia's house, they decided that after breakfast the next day they would say they were going for a walk, then run to the clearing where Violet would use her magic to take them to the marina.

"Hi, girls," Mia's dad said, appearing in the kitchen doorway as they arrived at Mia's house. He had an apron on, and his hands were floury. "I'm making homemade pizzas. Do you want to come and choose toppings?"

They shrugged off their coats and shoes and headed into the kitchen. Alex, Mia's little brother, was in his high chair, making shapes with pieces of leftover dough, while Mrs. Greene, Mia's mom, and Cleo, Mia's 15-year-old sister, were washing dishes. The girls set to work, getting the toppings ready to put on the pizzas.

"Do you remember your eighth birthday, Lexi, when you had a pizza-making party?" Sita said as she grated cheese.

"It was really funny," Lexi said to Violet, who hadn't been friends with her then. "We went to a pizza restaurant, and this chef was showing us how to stretch pizza dough. I tried to swirl mine around, and it flew out of my hands and went all over him!"

Mia's dad chuckled. "You've all had some fun birthday parties. You had a magician for your fifth birthday party, didn't you, Violet?'

Mia grinned. "I remember that. You kept getting upset with him because you said he wasn't doing the magic correctly."

"Well, he wasn't!" said Violet. "I could see the rabbit behind his table and the scarf stuffed up his sleeve!"

"It's strange to think that next year you might be having birthday parties with people you don't know—new friends from your middle schools," said Mrs. Greene.

"We'll still have our old friends, too," Mia replied quickly. She knew Lexi and Sita were

both a little anxious about starting school in
the fall, but for different reasons. Lexi was
worried about them staying friends because
she would be at a different school than the
others. She was going to Seaside High School,
whereas they would be at Oceanview Middle
School. Sita was nervous because she didn't
like anything changing. She didn't even like it
when they changed classes every year, so the
thought of starting at a new school was very
worrying.

Sita sighed. "I just know I'm going to get
lost when we start at Oceanview. I wish we
could stay at Westport forever."

"I don't," said Violet. "I'm looking forward
to changing schools. The science labs at
Oceanview look amazing!"

"My school has a math club and runs a math
Olympiad and math competitions," said Lexi.
"How cool is that?"

"Awesome!" said Violet.

"You two are seriously weird," said Mia with a grin. Both Violet and Lexi were very smart and loved academic competitions. She looked across at Sita and remembered what she'd been thinking about earlier. "Changing schools will be fine," she said. "Just because something's new and different doesn't mean it's going to be bad." She wished she could remind Sita that being a Star Friend had been a new thing for them last year, but she couldn't say that in front of her family.

"Mmm," Sita said, not sounding convinced.

"Mia's right, Sita," said Cleo, coming over. "I know it feels like a really big deal, but you get used to it very quickly. All the new sixth graders are assigned older buddies to help them find their way around for the first few weeks, so don't worry about getting lost, and the teachers will be nice to you—well, at first!"

Mrs. Greene nodded. "I'm sure after a few weeks you'll wonder why you were ever worried," she said.

"I'm ready to cook the pizzas!" said Mr. Greene. "Time to choose your toppings!"

They all started piling on the toppings. As Mia arranged pepperoni and peppers on hers, she pushed all thoughts of school out of her head. Right now, she was happy exactly where she was—getting ready for a homemade pizza feast with her friends and family, and having a fun magic adventure to look forward to in the morning!

5
A TRIP TO
THE MARINA

By nine o'clock that night, the girls were
snuggled up in their sleeping bags in Mia's
bedroom with their animals.

"I can't wait until the morning," said
Violet, petting Sorrel, who was stretched out
beside her, purring happily. "I hope we track
down Mystic Maureen so we can find out
more about the dolls and why she put the
Shades in them."

"Be careful," said Willow. She was beside
Sita, her slender legs curled underneath her.

"If this fortune-teller is the one doing dark magic, she might be dangerous."

"I wish we could come with you," said Bracken, nestling in Mia's bed to get closer to her.

She rubbed his ears. "I know, but I think people might ask questions if we arrived at the marina with a fox, a wildcat, a squirrel, and a deer!"

Juniper looked up from Lexi's pillow. "I hope you manage to solve the mystery of the Shades."

Mia felt a shiver of excitement run through her. She was really hoping that, too!

Mia felt like she had only just drifted off to sleep when she found herself in a vivid dream. Mystic Maureen was sitting at a table, peering at an old-fashioned phone, and Mia was standing behind her. On the phone screen she could see a picture of one of Mrs. Jefferson's dolls.

"You *did* do it!" Mia said to her. "You put the Shades in the dolls!"

But Mystic Maureen didn't hear her. "It'll help," she whispered to herself. "I'm sure it will."

What did she mean? Mia frowned, but just then, she heard angry voices, shouting, and banging. She turned. There was a doorway behind her. People were hammering on it and yelling. What was going on? They sounded furious.

The door started to splinter, and Mia turned to run....

Mia sat up in bed. The sky outside was still dark.

"Mia?" Bracken said.

"I was having a weird dream," she whispered, not wanting to disturb the others.

"A magic dream?" Bracken said with concern.

"I think so." Mia rubbed her forehead. "Mystic Maureen was in it. She was looking at a photo of one of Mrs. Jefferson's dolls on her phone. When she was at Mrs. Jefferson's house for the fortune-telling evening, I saw her taking photos of the dolls. It was a little weird."

"Was there anything else in your dream?" Bracken asked.

"Yes. There was a door, and there were people on the other side of it trying to get through—they sounded angry."

Bracken looked concerned. "I wonder what that means."

"I don't know, but it was scary," said Mia uneasily.

"The sooner you find this Mystic Maureen, the better," Bracken said, licking her hand comfortingly.

Mia hugged him. She was sure Mystic Maureen was the person who had conjured the Shades. They had to find her and stop her as soon as possible, and definitely before she used dark magic again. An image of the people banging on the door flashed back into her mind. Maybe that would actually happen if they didn't find Mystic Maureen in time....

The next morning, the girls had a quick breakfast and told Mrs. Greene they were going out. They raced to the clearing and gathered under a tree. Mia had shadow-traveled quite a few times with Violet, but it always felt weird. One minute she was standing in the shadows beside a tree with the others, and the next she felt the world slide away. It was like traveling in a very fast elevator. A second later, her feet hit pavement, and the four of them were now standing in a small alley.

At the end of the alley, they could see people walking past on a sunny street. There were babies in strollers, small children with fishing nets, and adults carrying beach towels. People's voices traveled toward them, but no one glanced in their direction.

"Time to find Mystic Maureen!" Violet said. "Come on!"

The others followed her out of the alley.

Seagulls were swooping across the blue sky, and the air smelled of seaweed and frying onions. On the other side of the wide street there was a harbor with moored boats, their sails folded. Farther along the street there were some souvenir and clothing stores, a small supermarket, and at the far end was a hotel with a large café beside it. The girls walked along the busy street, looking at all the stores and businesses. Then they checked the harbor where people were selling hot dogs and offering face-painting and hair-braiding. Finally, they reached the café.

"Maybe Mary got it wrong," Mia said, puzzled. "I thought we'd find a fortune-telling hut or something like that, but there's no sign of Mystic Maureen anywhere."

"Why don't we go and get an ice cream from the café?" said Lexi. "I have some money with me. We could ask the wait staff there if they've heard of Mystic Maureen."

They went into the bustling Friendly Fish
Café. The staff inside was rushed off their
feet serving people. The girls lined up for
ice-cream cones. When it was their turn to
be served, Mia asked the waitress if she had
heard of someone named Mystic Maureen.
"She's a fortune-teller," she added.

"I've never heard of anyone by that name,"
said the woman as she made up their cones.
"But if it's a fortune-teller you want, then

you should come back tomorrow." She handed out the ice-cream cones.

They took them and squeezed around a small table beside the counter. "I wonder what she meant about coming back tomorrow," Mia asked, but she was interrupted by the sound of a raised voice behind them.

An angry-looking man was telling off two of the waitresses. He had slicked-back gray hair and round eyes like a fish. "People are only allowed ketchup if they pay for it," he was saying sharply. "The same goes for mayonnaise. No freebies. Do you understand?"

"Yes, Mr. Hannigan," muttered the waitresses.

Mia stiffened. Hannigan? Where had she heard that name before?

"This place is really busy, isn't it?" said Sita.

"I don't know why," said Violet, wrinkling her nose. "This ice cream is nowhere near as good as Mary's. It tastes really artificial and," she half stood up to peer at the counter, "those cakes look like they've been there for a few days."

The man scolding the waitresses overheard her. "I'll have you know that all of our cakes here at the Friendly Fish Café are freshly made!" he said.

"Well, your ice cream doesn't taste very good." Violet loved an argument and pointed to a sign by the ice-cream counter. "Is it really homemade? It doesn't taste like it is."

The man's eyes bulged angrily. "What?"

Mia noticed that people around them had started to listen in. Violet seemed to have noticed, too.

"The Copper Kettle's ice cream is much better," she said loudly.

Mia hid a grin. She knew exactly what Violet was doing. Maybe the people who heard her would now try Mary's café instead!

"Absolute nonsense! Now get out of here! You can't take up a table if you're just having ice cream anyway. Tables are for meals only!" snapped the man.

"Come on, Violet," said Sita, who hated scenes and shouting.

"Fine, we'll go. We'll just head on back to THE COPPER KETTLE!" Violet said, almost shouting the name. "They're very friendly there!"

"Violet!" Sita exclaimed to Violet as they left. "That man was really angry with you."

"So?" said Violet.

"He was mean," said Lexi.

Mia suddenly remembered where she had heard the man's name before. "I know who he is! He's the person who doesn't like Mr. Jefferson—Desmond Hannigan. He owns the marina."

"If he doesn't like Mr. Jefferson, he's definitely a horrible person," said Lexi. "Mr. Jefferson is really nice. I guess Mr. Hannigan could be a suspect," she went on. "He could have put the Shades in the dolls."

Mia pictured Mr. Hannigan. He really hadn't looked like the kind of person who would do magic. "Mystic Maureen seems much more likely. I saw her with the dolls, and the magic hasn't shown me Mr. Hannigan at all."

"I guess that's true," Lexi conceded.

"If only we could find her!" said Mia. She went to put the remains of her cone in a nearby garbage can. As she did, she saw a poster stuck to a bulletin board:

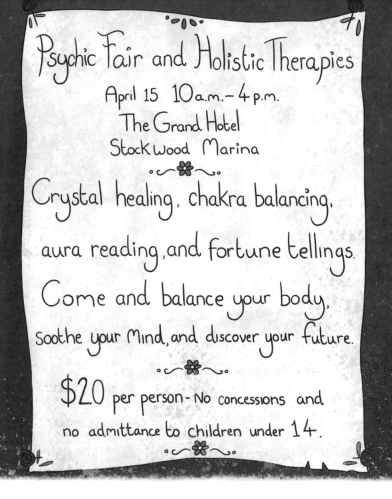

Psychic Fair and Holistic Therapies

April 15   10 a.m. – 4 p.m.
The Grand Hotel
Stock Wood Marina

Crystal healing, chakra balancing,

aura reading, and fortune tellings.

Come and balance your body,

soothe your mind, and discover your future.

$20 per person – No concessions and

no admittance to children under 14.

Mia gasped. April 15 was the following day! That must have been what the waitress meant when she said they should come back tomorrow if they wanted a fortune-teller.

"Look!" She pointed to the notice.

"We have to go!" said Violet. "If it's a

psychic fair with fortune-telling, Mystic Maureen will probably be there."

"But it's really expensive, and it says you have to be fourteen," said Sita.

Mia thought for a moment. She certainly didn't have twenty dollars, and none of them looked fourteen, so even if Violet shadow-traveled them inside, they'd probably be asked to leave.

Violet giggled suddenly. "Hang on, I think I might just have an idea!" she said, her green eyes shining. "How about—"

"Violet!" squeaked Lexi in alarm, pointing behind her. "It's your dad!"

Violet's dad was heading down the street toward them. He was skirting around a group of parents with toddlers and hadn't noticed them yet. "Quick! We're not supposed to be at the marina. Hide!" Mia gasped.

6
A PLAN

The girls dove into a nearby souvenir shop and watched from inside as Violet's dad walked down the street.

"We'd better go home in case he sees us," said Mia. "Come on—quick! While he's heading the other way!"

They hurried to the alley and stepped into the shadows beside the garbage cans.

"I'll take us back to the clearing," said Violet. "We can call the animals, and I'll tell you my idea for tomorrow. Hold hands!"

They grabbed hands. The alley vanished into shadows, and they were swept away.

As their feet touched solid ground, Mia breathed in the earthy smell of trees and leaves. Birds twittered in the branches, and a wild gray squirrel was looking down at them curiously from a tree.

They called their animals' names. In the blink of an eye, the four Star Animals appeared. Bracken and Juniper bounded into Mia and Lexi's arms. Willow cantered playfully around the clearing, and Sorrel wove around Violet's legs, purring loudly. After they had all said hello, the girls sat down by the waterfall and told the animals everything that had happened.

"So, we might not have found Mystic Maureen today, but Violet has an idea for how we can get into the fortune-telling fair tomorrow," finished Mia.

"It isn't how *we* can get in, but how *I* can get in," said Violet. "Watch."

The air shimmered around her, and suddenly she changed into an elderly lady with gray hair in a bun and deep wrinkles around her mouth and eyes. She was wearing a long red skirt and had a black shawl around her shoulders. She rubbed her hands together. "Who'd like Psychic Sue to do a reading for them at the fair tomorrow? Would you, my dear?" She shuffled over to Mia. "Show me your palm, and I'll tell you your future!"

Mia squealed in delight. "Violet! That's incredible!"

Sorrel purred like she was going to explode. "Oh, you amazing girl!" she said. "What a genius use of your magic!"

"You're really planning on going to the fair and pretending to be a fortune-teller?" said Sita, wide-eyed.

Violet/Psychic Sue nodded. "I've been practicing disguising myself using a glamour, and now I can put it to good use," she said in her normal voice.

"But what if the disguise fails and that Mr. Hannigan is there at the hotel and sees you?" said Lexi.

"It won't fail," Violet said confidently. She transformed back into herself. "So, what do you think?"

"I think it's perfect!" said Mia, high-fiving her. Lexi and Sita were looking slightly worried, but Mia just felt envious. "I wish I could come with you."

"You can watch me using your own magic

and tell the others what's happening," said
Violet. She beamed. "Let's meet here in the
morning, and I'll shadow-travel there then.
Agreed?"

"Agreed!" they all said.

However, later that day, there was a change of
plan. Mia and Alex were playing with his trains
on the kitchen floor when her phone pinged.
It was a message from Violet to all of them.

> Hi. Dad was at the marina today cos he wanted
> 2 have a look around and see what it was like.
> He says he'll take us all 2moro if we want to go.
> I think we can still do what we were planning!
> Vxxx

Mia smiled. The girls tried to be very
careful with what they put in messages in
case any of their parents ever looked at their
phones.

"Mom, can I go to the new marina with

Violet and the others tomorrow?" she asked, looking up. "Violet's dad is going to take us."

"Sure," her mom said.

Mia texted Violet back.

> I can come! What time? xx

> Dad says he'll pick u up at 9:30! Bring bathing suits and towels cos we're going 2 go 2 the water park. Fun and you-know-what! Vx

You-know-what was their code for magic. Mia sent Violet smiley and winky faces back.

Just then the door opened, and her dad and Cleo came in. "Look what we picked up at the Copper Kettle!" he said. "Chocolate cake!" He opened the cake box to reveal a cake covered with chocolate fudge frosting.

"Mmm," said Mia, her mouth watering. It looked delicious.

"I thought we could have it for dessert tonight," her dad said.

"I can't. I'm trying to be more healthy," said Cleo.

"Just a little piece," Dad said, waving the cake temptingly under her nose.

Cleo groaned. "Don't be mean, Dad!"

"Cake!" Alex said, looking up. "Want cake!"

Mia's mom smiled. "All right, you can have a piece of cake, then it's time to brush teeth and go to bed."

She cut a little slice. Alex ate it greedily. "More!" His eyes widened. "Pleeeeease!"

"Just a little bit." Mia's mom handed him a second piece and licked her fingers. "It is very good."

"It's a new recipe," said Mia, using her finger to pick up a few crumbs of sponge and frosting from the box. It really was delicious.

"Want more cake! More!" Alex cried.

Mr. Greene laughed. "No more now, Alex. It's bedtime."

Alex started to kick and scream as his dad picked him up. "Oh, dear," said Mia's mom, rolling her eyes at the girls as Alex was carried out of the kitchen. "I think someone's very overtired tonight. Now let's set the table for dinner."

As Mia got out the cutlery, she thought about the next day. Hopefully, they would get to meet Mystic Maureen. She felt a flutter of excitement. Maybe tomorrow they were finally going to get some real answers!

7
VIOLET GOES TO THE
PSYCHIC FAIR

The next morning, Violet's dad drove them all to the marina. "Who's ready to go in the swimming pool?" he said as they parked and got out.

"Actually, Dad, could we shop a little first?" asked Violet.

"Sure," her dad said. "If you want to take a look around, I'll go to the café. See you in a bit!" And he left them to it.

"Okay, this is my chance," whispered Violet when he was gone. "I'll go into the changing room in one of the shops, disguise myself, and then shadow-travel into the fair at the hotel."

"Meanwhile, we'll watch you with my magic!" Mia said.

"Don't do anything dangerous!" said Lexi.

Violet grinned. "Me? Never!" She winked at them and headed into a nearby clothing store.

The others found a bench in a quiet spot by the harbor wall, away from all of the crowds and from Violet's dad. Mia cradled the mirror in her hands. "Show me Violet," she said.

As she connected with the magic, the surface of the mirror glimmered, and an image of a lady with gray hair, a long red skirt, and a black shawl around her shoulders appeared. Only her green eyes were recognizably Violet's. "I can see her! She looks amazing," Mia told the others.

"Where is she?" asked Lexi.

"In a big room inside the hotel," Mia

answered, her eyes scanning the picture. "It has a high ceiling and a lot of people inside. There are people sitting behind tables, selling things." Mia read a few of the signs propped up on the tables: aura reading, mystical books, moon-blessed herbs....

A shiver ran down her spine as she read that sign. She knew it was possible for people to learn how to harness the power in plants and herbs to do magic. Some people used that kind of magic to do good, but she and the others had once had to stop someone evil who was using plant magic to upset people.

"What's Violet doing?" asked Sita anxiously.

"She's just walking around." Mia could tell Violet was enjoying being in disguise. She was smiling at people, nodding and stopping to chat with some of the vendors.

A girl of about eighteen with pink hair came up to her and asked her something. Mia focused on the picture in the mirror until she could hear what was being said.

"So, you're really a fortune-teller?" the girl was saying to Violet.

"Yes, my dear," Violet replied. "I can pull back the veil of the future and see beyond it to what will come."

Mia grinned.

The girl's eyes widened. "Will you look into my future?"

Violet took the girl's hand and stared at it for a long moment. "Elephants!" she announced suddenly. "I see elephants in your future!"

Mia started to giggle. What was Violet doing?

"Elephants?" echoed the girl. "Wow! That's so weird. I love elephants. How did you know?"

"Magic," said Violet, but Mia saw her eyes flick to the silver elephant necklace and earrings the girl was wearing. "You must travel far to see them, and you will do a lot of good!"

"That's awesome! I've been trying to decide where to go after I graduate and before college. Now I know!" said the girl. "I'll go to Sri Lanka and help at an elephant orphanage. Thank you so much!" She hurried off, smiling. Violet hid a grin.

"What's happening?" said Sita as Mia chuckled.

"Violet's having fun." Mia told them about the girl, while still keeping an eye on Violet, who was now talking to one of the fortune-tellers sitting behind a table. "She's heading for the door now," she said, watching as Violet left. "She's going down a hallway. I think she's looking for somewhere she can go to travel back." She saw Violet look around and check that she was alone before stepping into a patch of shadows and vanishing. "Yes, she's coming back!"

"Let's go and meet her," said Sita.

They reached the store just as Violet came out. "That was so much fun!" She grabbed Mia's hands in excitement.

"Excuse me, what do you think you're doing?" They all swung around at the sound of Violet's dad's voice. He walked over, frowning. "Please leave these girls alone."

Violet had been in such a rush that she'd forgotten to change back into herself! To Mia's horror, Violet didn't hurry off. She just ducked her head so her dad couldn't see her eyes and grabbed his hand. "I could read your fortune, kind sir. Psychic Sue is never wrong."

"Um…uh…." Mr. Cooper looked like he didn't know what to do.

"A-ha, I see you have a very intelligent daughter with red hair," said Violet in her croaky, elderly-lady voice. "Yes, I can see her here in your palm. She is very smart indeed, and she deserves a bigger allowance."

Mr. Cooper blinked. "What?"

"I really think you should go now, Psychic Sue," said Mia hastily as Lexi tried to hold back her laughter and snorted loudly.

"I will be back," declared Violet. "Mark my words! And remember, Psychic Sue is never wrong!" With that, she hurried away, disappearing into the crowd of people on the streets.

Mr. Cooper shook his head. "What an eccentric woman!" He looked around. "Where's Violet, girls?"

"Um, really close by," said Lexi truthfully.

"I think she went into one of the stores to try something on," said Sita.

Just then Violet came jogging over, looking like her usual eleven-year-old self. "Here she is!" Mia said.

Violet skipped over to them. "Thanks for waiting for me! Hi, Dad."

"Violet, I don't want you going off on your

own," said her dad. "There are some very strange people around."

"Really?" said Violet innocently. "Okay, we'll stick together from now on."

"Let's get your swimming things and go to the water park," said her dad.

They followed him back to the car. "What did you find out at the fair?" Mia asked quietly.

"I'll tell you when we're on our own," Violet whispered back.

They had to wait until they were in the girls' changing rooms before they were alone. They huddled together in a single cubicle. "I can't believe you tried to tell your dad's fortune!" Sita whispered to Violet.

"I know! Did you see his face?" Violet grinned.

"It was very funny!" Mia said.

"Did you find out anything about Mystic

Maureen?" Lexi demanded.

"Well, she wasn't there, and none of the other fortune-tellers had ever heard of her," said Violet. "The last lady I spoke to said she knew everyone in the area who worked as a fortune-teller, and she'd never heard of a Mystic Maureen."

"How weird!" said Mia.

Lexi looked thoughtful. "Unless Mystic Maureen isn't a real fortune-teller. Maybe she was just pretending for the PTSA night."

They considered that, but then Violet shook her head. "No. If that were the case, why would she have business cards at the Copper Kettle?"

"True," Lexi admitted.

"So, what do we do now?" asked Mia. "My dreams and magic visions are all telling me that Mystic Maureen put the Shades in Mrs. Jefferson's dolls, and hinting that something else bad is going to happen, but how do we find her?"

None of them knew.

"This is making my head hurt," groaned Sita. "I vote we go swimming and forget about it for a while."

The water park was so much fun with twisting slides, a wave machine, and warm tropical pools. Afterward, they had a picnic lunch and then played baseball on the beach. It was almost a relief just to be normal and to forget about the mystery of Mystic Maureen, but when Mia was in her bedroom that night, she talked about it with Bracken.

"I just don't get it," she said as they lay on her bed. "Why has no one heard of Mystic Maureen? It's like she just vanished into thin air."

"It is very strange." He put his head on her tummy.

"Don't!" she said with a groan. "I ate too

much for dinner."

Her mom had been back to the Copper Kettle and come home with a lemon drizzle cake. The lemon drizzle had been just as delicious as the chocolate cake—soft sponge oozing with sweet lemon frosting. Mia had had three big slices, and now she was feeling sick!

Bracken rolled over onto his back. Mia tickled his belly. "I don't know what else we can do to find her."

Her phone buzzed, and she picked it up. There was a group message from Lexi.

"Listen to this," Mia breathed. She read the message to Bracken. *"I've just had one of my weird feelings again! I was falling asleep when I suddenly felt scared, like something horrible was going to happen. This is just like last time when the Shades appeared. Something dangerous is coming. I know it."*

"That's not good," Bracken said anxiously. "Do you think more Shades are going to appear in Westport?"

Mia thought about the dream she'd had about the furious people trying to break a door down. Shades made people angry and behave in strange ways. "Maybe." She texted Lexi and the others back.

We need 2 be careful. Let's meet 2moro and decide what 2 do then. Mxx

OK. About 10? Sxx

I can't. I'm out in the morning with Mom. Vx

I have a tennis lesson in the morning, too. How about we meet at 2 p.m. in the clearing? Lxx

Mia typed back.

OK. But cd u and I meet earlier, Sita? We cd meet at my house and go 2 the clearing.

Sita sent a smiley face and a thumbs up back.

Don't do ANYTHING without us!!!!! Vxxx

We won't. Night! Mxx

She put her phone down. "We're all going to meet tomorrow afternoon," she told Bracken.

"Good," said Bracken. "Then we can come up with a plan about what to do next."

Mia nodded and yawned. "I really hope I don't have bad dreams tonight," she said, flopping back against the pillow.

He snuggled closer. "I'll be here if you do."

She kissed his nose and fell asleep with him curled up in her arms.

8
A Busy Copper Kettle

To Mia's relief, all she dreamed about was cake. She was sitting in the Copper Kettle, eating one cake after another. It was much better than dreaming about Shades! She woke up, her tummy rumbling.

"After last night, I thought I wouldn't want to eat again for a whole day," she said to Bracken as she got up. "But I'm really hungry now! I'm going to get some breakfast."

However, once she was downstairs,

she couldn't find anything that appealed to her. Not cereal, not oatmeal, not toast. She shut the cupboard door with a loud bang.

"Are you okay?" her dad asked.

"I don't know what I want to eat," she said.

"I'm feeling like that, too," he admitted. "How about I make bacon and eggs?"

Mia really loved hot breakfasts, so she nodded.

Her dad made the food, but when Mia started eating it, she quickly lost her appetite. She ate half the plateful and then put her knife and fork down. "I'm sorry, Dad. I guess I'm not that hungry."

"Don't worry." Her dad was pushing his food unenthusiastically around his plate. "I thought I wanted this, but now I'm not so sure. Maybe we're both coming down with something."

Mia nodded, and after putting her plate in the dishwasher, she went back upstairs, feeling strangely grumpy.

At 10 o'clock, Sita arrived, and they headed for the clearing, talking about the strange feeling Lexi had had the night before.

"Do you think it means more Shades are going to appear?" Sita asked anxiously.

"I don't know," said Mia. "We may be in

danger from some other type of dark magic."

She saw the worried expression on Sita's face and squeezed her arm. "It'll be okay. We've fought people using dark magic before, and we've always won."

Sita nodded. "I'm so glad we're Star Friends and get to do magic together."

"I know," said Mia. "I was thinking the other day how much everything has changed since we found out about the Star World." She shot Sita a sideways look, seeing a chance to reassure her about starting school. "Change doesn't have to be bad, you know. New things can be good—really good! Like learning how to do magic."

Sita was quiet for a moment. "I hadn't thought about it like that before," she admitted.

"Imagine if we'd never met the Star Animals, and our lives had stayed just like they were before we met them," Mia went on. "There's no way you would want that, is there?"

Sita shook her head firmly. "No! Being a Star Friend is the best thing that's ever happened to me. I couldn't bear to be without Willow now."

Mia felt the same about Bracken. "So, you see, change can be good," she said.

Sita nodded. "I guess." She glanced at her friend. "Are you worried about the state tests?"

"Kind of," Mia admitted. "Mom and Dad say they don't mind how I do as long as I try my best, but Cleo did well on hers, and I don't want to mess them up."

"A whole week of exams!" said Sita. "It's going to be horrible."

"Let's not think about it now," said Mia as they turned onto the main street. "The Copper Kettle looks busy today," she said. "There are a bunch of people inside."

She could see a line of people at the counter. Mary and her assistant, Rebecca, were rushing around, delivering food and quickly cleaning up as people left so others could sit down.

"I bet it's because of the new cakes!" said Mia, feeling really happy for Mary. "We had one last night, and they're so yummy." She felt in her pocket. Her mom had given her her allowance the day before. "I've got enough for a slice each. Should we go in?"

"Okay," said Sita eagerly. "I had some of the new cake yesterday. My grandma brought a sponge cake over to our house for dessert."

"You have to try the chocolate cake— and the lemon drizzle," said Mia. "They're amazing!"

They went in and joined the line.

"The cakes in here are just so delicious," Mia heard a woman at a nearby table say. "So much better than the ones at the Friendly Fish."

"Yes," her companion said. "I heard people talking about them at the marina yesterday and thought I had to come and try them out." She scraped the crumbs off her plate with her fork. "I'm going to be taking some home, that's for sure!"

Mia felt a warm glow. She was really happy that people were realizing how much better Mary's cakes were than those at the marina café. Maybe Violet's little outburst yesterday had worked! Desmond Hannigan wouldn't be happy....

"Excuse me! Can we get another slice of carrot cake over here, please?" a man called, holding his hand in the air.

"With you in a minute!" Mary called back, looking flustered as she rang up a customer's bill. "I'm sorry about the wait," she apologized to the long line of people standing at the counter. "I'll just be one moment."

"Coffee and walnut cake, three slices of carrot cake, and a scone?" called Rebecca, coming through from the kitchen.

"That's for us!" called Margaret, one of Mia's grandmother's friends, who was sitting at a table with a group of ladies from church.

"They really do need to get more staff in here," the woman in front of Mia muttered.

"We could offer to help," Mia said to Sita.

Sita nodded. "Yes, sure!"

Mary was delighted with the offer. "Thank you, girls. I could really do with some help cleaning tables and carrying plates. Rebecca and I are run off our feet!"

"We're free all morning," said Mia. "Just tell us what you want us to do."

The girls washed their hands in the kitchen and then set to work. Everyone certainly seemed to be enjoying the food.

"It's great that you have so many people in here," Mia said to Mary as she helped her bring some new cakes through from the kitchen and put them under the counter.

Mary picked up a battered leather book from the side. "It's all thanks to Grandma's special recipes in here!"

There was a crash on the other side of the counter. Mia and Mary looked around. A man sitting at a nearby table had stood up and knocked his chair into Sita as she'd been passing with a slice of cake on a plate. Mia had noticed him earlier because he'd been behaving a little strangely. He had kept a hat on that hid his face, and he'd been taking pictures of the menu on his phone. He'd also been eating ice cream, which she had thought was a little odd for a cold and gray morning.

"I'm sorry!" Sita gasped, looking at the mess on the floor. "I didn't realize you were about to stand up."

"You clearly weren't looking where you were going!" the man snapped. His voice sounded familiar.

"Don't worry, Sita," said Mary. "Are you okay, sir? Did any cake get on you? Do you need a napkin?" But the man had left some money on the table and was already hurrying out of the café.

When he was outside, he looked back, and
Mia realized who he was. Desmond Hannigan!
But what was he doing in the Copper Kettle,
and why had he been acting so peculiarly?
He hurried away and got into a shiny black car.

Mia began clearing the table, her
mind turning over the fact that Desmond
Hannigan had been there. He didn't seem
like the kind of person who would just come
into the Copper Kettle for an ice cream.
A nagging thought wormed its way into
her mind. Their other magic adventures
had taught her to take notice when people
behaved strangely, and this certainly seemed
strange! Could Desmond Hannigan possibly
have something to do with the dark magic
after all? The magic hadn't shown her any
pictures of him, and he didn't look like the
kind of person who would do magic. But he
didn't like Mr. Jefferson, and the Star Friends
had been tricked by people before.

No, she thought. *Surely Mystic Maureen has to be responsible.*

She picked up a newspaper from a table and put it in the wooden rack beside the door. As she did so, she spotted a multicolored scarf hanging on the coat rack. She caught her breath. It was the same scarf Mystic Maureen had been wearing the night of the fortune-telling event! She swung around. Was Mystic Maureen here right now?

Heart beating fast, Mia studied all of the people in the café. But there was no one who looked anything like the fortune-teller.

"Are you okay?" Mary said, pausing beside her.

Mia realized she must look odd, staring around wildly. "Yes, I'm…. I'm fine," she said and hurried off to clean another table. But her mind was racing. Mystic Maureen must have been in the café and left her scarf there. If that were the case, then hopefully she'd come back and get it soon! *Then we'll finally get the chance to talk to her,* Mia thought.

9
Strange Behaviors

Mia and Sita helped until it was time to meet the others. Mary had made them a sandwich for lunch, and she gave them a large slice of carrot cake each to take with them. To Mia's disappointment, Mystic Maureen hadn't come back to claim her scarf.

They ate their cake as they walked to the clearing to meet the others. Seeing Violet and Lexi just ahead of them on the road, they hurried to catch up.

"Hi!" called Lexi. "What have you two

been up to?"

"Helping at the Copper Kettle and eating cake." Mia grinned as she saw the surprise on Lexi and Violet's faces. "We'll tell you all about it when we have the animals, too. I think I might have found something that will help us track down Mystic Maureen!"

When they were in the clearing with their animals, Mia told them about the scarf.

"Mystic Maureen must have been in there," she finished. "And if she left her scarf there, she's hopefully going to go back."

"We have to keep watch at the café for her!" Violet said.

Juniper flicked his bushy tail. "I wonder if she has anything to do with the feeling Lexi had last night that danger is heading our way."

"Indeed," Sorrel said, rubbing her head against Violet's fingers. "Mia, did you dream about anything last night?"

"Just eating cake in the Copper Kettle,"

Mia said. "No Shades. Nothing magic."

"The Copper Kettle again." Sorrel sat down thoughtfully and flicked her tail around her paws. "Maybe the new danger is going to appear there. After all, the scarf does suggest that the fortune-teller has visited the café recently."

"She could have left an object in there with a Shade inside it," said Juniper. "Maybe even that scarf itself!"

"Did you see anything unusual in the café this morning?" asked Bracken.

"No," said Sita. "Nothing. There were just a lot of customers."

"There was one thing," Mia remembered. "Desmond Hannigan was there."

"The man who owns the marina?" said Lexi. "The man who was telling off those waitresses yesterday?"

"Yes," answered Mia. "And the man who doesn't like Mr. Jefferson. He was in the Copper

Kettle this morning acting really strangely."

"What was he doing?" asked Willow curiously.

"He had his face hidden as if he didn't want to be recognized, and he was taking pictures of the menu," said Mia.

"He left really quickly," said Sita. "He made me drop some cake! What a waste!" She sighed. "You know, I wouldn't mind some more of Mary's cake right now."

"Me, too," said Mia, her tummy rumbling at the thought.

"You both just had some!" said Violet.

"I know, but it's so yummy," said Mia, thinking wistfully of the carrot cake.

"We have much more important things to think about than cake!" Sorrel said sharply. "What you've told us isn't much to go on. Maybe this man—"

"Wait!" Lexi exclaimed. Sorrel swished her tail, looking annoyed at being interrupted. "What did you just say, Sita? A few minutes ago. When Sorrel asked if there was anything unusual at the café, you said no, just a lot of customers. Don't you see?" She looked at them all. "That's something unusual! The Copper Kettle hasn't had many customers, and then suddenly it's really busy. Maybe Mystic Maureen has put more Heart's Desire Shades somewhere in the café, and they're granting Mary's wish for more customers, just like they granted Mr. Jefferson's wish that Westport would win the Prettiest Small Town competition."

"Great thought, Lexi!" burst out Juniper.

"Yes! You could be right! Shades could be making people come in and eat Mary's food!" Sita exclaimed.

Sorrel spluttered. "Don't be ridiculous! Shades make people angry, jealous, unhappy, and scared—they don't make people want to eat cake! If Shades were involved, I think we'd see something more dramatic happening."

Sita's face fell. "Oh."

Willow nuzzled her hand. "Sorrel's right," she said gently. "Eating Mary's food clearly makes her customers happy, and Shades don't like people being happy, so it's unlikely that Shades are making them eat Mary's food." She frowned. "But it is odd that there are so many people all of a sudden."

"I think we should check if there are Shades in the café," said Bracken.

Sorrel nodded. "I'll go there now and see

what I can find out."

Some Star Animals, like Sorrel and Willow, could smell when Shades had been nearby.

"Come back soon," said Violet. Sorrel touched her nose to Violet's and vanished.

They waited anxiously. Mia chewed a fingernail. Had someone put Shades in the café? Was dark magic involved? Mia shivered. What if something happened to Mary, and she couldn't make cakes anymore?

After a little while, Sorrel reappeared. "There are no Shades," she said, relief in her indigo eyes. "In fact, there was nothing of any note at the café, except for all of the people in there." She sniffed indignantly. "One of them almost stepped on my tail!"

"So, no Shades, but some dark magic could still be going on there," said Violet. "Someone could be using plant or crystal magic."

"But then we're back to the fact that nothing bad is happening there," said Lexi.

"Yet," said Sorrel darkly. "I definitely think you need to watch this café closely. Something may happen soon."

"We could all offer to help there this afternoon," said Sita.

Sorrel nodded. "Keep your eyes and ears open."

"And be careful," added Willow.

"We will," the girls promised.

The Copper Kettle was teeming with customers when they went back, and Mary was very glad to accept the girls' offer of help. To their disappointment, Mystic Maureen did not reappear to claim her scarf, and nothing unusual happened at all. By mid-afternoon, all of the cakes were gone, and Mary closed early. There were some new customers getting out of a car as the girls left.

"We've driven half an hour to get here,"

said one of the men. "We came yesterday afternoon, and you were open until five then."

"I'm terribly sorry, but we've completely sold out of food today, and I really need to close now so I can do some more baking," Mary said, looking flustered.

"I'm going to be up all night," she said to the girls as the people got back into their car, looking annoyed. "I like it being busy, but not this busy. Thanks so much for all of your help today."

When Mia opened the front door and walked in, she smelled the delicious sweet aroma of cake. "Mmm," she said, going into the kitchen.

There was a freshly baked chocolate cake on the table. Cleo was decorating it with frosting and chocolate sprinkles. "Mom really wanted some cake at lunchtime, so I thought I'd do some baking," she said.

"Yum! Can I have some?" Mia asked eagerly.

"No. It's for dessert when everyone's here," said Cleo.

Mia scowled. "But I want cake now!"

"Have a cookie instead," said Cleo, looking taken aback.

Mia took a cookie and stomped upstairs. She flung herself down on her bed, feeling very grumpy. *I'm just tired,* she thought. *It's been a busy day.*

By five o'clock, everyone except for Mr. Greene was home, and Cleo let them have some cake. Mia took a huge mouthful, and a wave of disappointment washed over her. It wasn't as good as the cake from the Copper Kettle. She put the slice down and pushed her plate away.

Mrs. Greene did the same with an annoyed exclamation.

"What's the matter?" said Cleo in surprise. "Don't you like it?" She had taken a break from her healthy eating to have a slice.

"No. I don't like!" said Alex grouchily.
"Want diff'rent cake!"

"But this is a special cake I just made!" said
Cleo. She used a fork to pick some up from his
plate. "Come on, Alex. Yum-yum!"

"Yuck! Yuck!" he said, knocking her hand
away and sending the cake and
his plastic plate flying onto
the floor.

"Alex! That's naughty!"
Mrs. Greene snapped.

"Want diff'rent cake!"
Alex started to
scream as she
lifted him
out of his
high chair.

"Want it now!"
He drummed his fists and
heels against her.

"You're going to your

bedroom!" Mrs. Greene said sharply, and she carried him upstairs still screaming. "Oh, don't be such a naughty boy!" she exclaimed.

Mia blinked. Her mom was usually really patient. She turned and saw Cleo's face. She looked really upset. "It's good cake, Cleo," Mia said, forcing her own annoyance down. "It's really delicious." She finished her slice but put her plate in the dishwasher before Cleo could offer her another piece. She wished her mom had bought a cake from the Copper Kettle.

Mia went up to her room. She called Bracken, and he jumped on the bed beside her.

"Are you all right?" he asked.

She shrugged. "I'm in a bad mood. I don't know why—I just don't feel right."

Bracken snuggled up to her. "You've had a busy day, and there's been a lot to think about."

She petted him and felt her grumpiness start to lift. It was impossible to be in a bad mood when she had him beside her. "What do you think's going on, Bracken?"

He licked her hand. "I don't know, but whatever it is, we'll find out and stop it."

Mia nodded. She shut her eyes, thoughts jumping around in her head: the Shades in the dolls ... Mystic Maureen ... the Copper Kettle ... all of the people there ... Lexi's feeling that they were in danger ... the angry people in her dream....

What did it all mean? She had the frustrating feeling that she had all the pieces of the puzzle, but she just couldn't get them to fit together, and as she was trying to figure it out, a hidden menace was edging closer and closer.

10
An Odd Dream Come True!

Mia was on the street across from the Copper Kettle in her pajamas. It was still night, although the sky was just starting to lighten in the east. A movement caught her eye. A very tall, thin man in dark clothes and a balaclava was creeping up to the bay window. She saw him raise one hand and realized he was holding a brick.

SMASH! The brick shattered the window.

Mia's feet were rooted to the spot. The café alarm started to scream out as the thief climbed into the café. A minute later, he came out, carrying two large cake boxes. He ran away down the street....

Mia woke up in bed, her heart pounding.

"Mia?" said Bracken, sitting up, too, his fur ruffled.

Mia glanced at the clock. It was six a.m. "I was dreaming about the Copper Kettle. I saw someone breaking in, only it didn't feel like a dream. It felt real!" She pushed the covers off and jumped out of bed. "I need to go and see what's happening!"

She started pulling on her clothes.

"What about your parents?" Bracken said.

"I'll leave them a note saying I've gone out for a walk," said Mia. "Oh, Bracken, I hope Mary's okay—she lives above the café."

"Be careful!" he said anxiously as she pulled open her bedroom door.

Mia ran through the peaceful streets of Westport. Dawn was breaking, and the birds were singing. The streets were deserted, but as she turned onto the main road, she saw Mary standing outside the Copper Kettle, looking at a broken window. Mia sprinted over.

"Mary, are you all right? What happened?"

Mary looked shocked. "I was asleep when suddenly I heard the sound of breaking glass, and then the alarm went off. Someone broke into the café! Thank goodness I had my grandma's journal upstairs with me so they couldn't steal that, and they didn't take any of my antique teddy bears or dolls."

"So, what *did* they steal?" asked
Mia.

"Just some cakes," said Mary. "I'd put
them under the counter for when I opened
this morning, and now they're gone. The
strange thing is, the intruder put them in
boxes and left money on the counter."

Mia blinked. The thief had paid for them!

"Oh, this is awful," said Mary, looking
close to tears. "I guess I'd better get this
glass swept up and call someone to come and
repair the window." She gave Mia a puzzled
look. "What are you doing out at this hour?"

"Just taking an early-morning walk," said
Mia. "I can help you clean up."

She and Mary began sweeping up the glass.

"Are you going to make some more
cakes?" Mia asked hungrily, looking at the
space under the counter where the stolen
cakes had been displayed.

"Luckily I have some more in the back,"

said Mary.

"Can I have a slice?" Mia asked eagerly.

"For breakfast? I don't think your mom would approve," said Mary with a smile. "How about one of my breakfast muffins instead?"

She fetched Mia a muffin. "Thanks," Mia said, her heart sinking as she took the muffin. She didn't know why, but she just really felt like eating cake and nothing else. "I'd better go home now. I hope you get the window fixed."

Mia walked back, munching on the muffin. It was tasty, but nowhere near as good as one of Mary's cakes.

"Where have you been?" her mom asked as she went in through the front door.

"Didn't you see my note? I went for a walk. I was passing the Copper Kettle, and guess what? It was broken into last night! Someone stole Mary's cakes."

"There are some left, aren't there?" her mom said apprehensively. Mia nodded.

"Phew!" Her mom looked relieved. "I was going to buy us one for dessert."

"Don't wait too long," said Mia. "Mary sold out of everything yesterday by mid-afternoon, and I have to have some more cake today!" Her mouth watered at the thought of eating Mary's chocolate cake. She wished she could have some right now!

"Who breaks into a café to steal cakes?" said Violet when they were all sitting in her bedroom later that morning, their animals beside them.

"And leaves money for them," Lexi pointed out. "Why not just wait until the café opens?"

"It's so weird," said Sita. "Though I would really like some cake right now."

Willow nuzzled her. "I told you that you should have had some breakfast."

Sita shrugged. "I didn't feel like cereal. I just wanted cake."

"You didn't have breakfast, either, did you, Mia?" said Bracken, nudging her with his nose.

"No." Mia had looked in the cupboards and fridge, but just like the day before, nothing had really appealed to her. Hunger pangs were now gnawing at her stomach, making her feel grouchy.

"Have you tried using your magic to see who the thief was, Mia?" Violet asked.

Mia was too busy picturing a chocolate cake to reply.

"Earth to Mia!" said Violet, waving a hand in front of her friend's face.

"What?" said Mia.

"Weren't you listening to me? I said, why don't you use magic to see what happened at the café?" Violet said impatiently.

Mia scowled. She didn't want to do magic.
All she really wanted to do was eat cake,
but she saw that everyone was looking at her
expectantly.

She took out her mirror. They really
should find out who had broken in and stolen
the cakes. She pictured the
cakes that had been
taken, and her
tummy rumbled
loudly. *Mmm.*
Chocolate
cake....

"Mia!" Lexi
exclaimed. "What
are you doing?"

Mia realized she
was staring into space
again. "Oh ... um
... sorry." She forced

her mind to concentrate and connected to the magic current. "Show me who stole the cakes," she said to the mirror.

The magic showed her a tall, thin man dressed all in black, just as she had seen in her dream. He threw a brick through the window of the café. "Show me the thief's face," Mia said, but although the magic zoomed in, the man's face was hidden by a woolly balaclava pulled over his head.

"I can't see who the thief is," she said. "It looks a little like Mr. Jefferson, judging by the size and shape, but it can't be. He'd never break in anywhere." She watched as the thief climbed in through the window and then reappeared, carrying two large cake boxes. Where had those cakes gone? Had the thief eaten them? Might there be some left? Mia's mouth watered, and then she realized the image had vanished from the mirror.

"You know, I think I really need some

cake," she said, jumping to her feet.

"Cake?" Violet echoed.

"Yes, right now."

"Me, too," said Sita, getting up. "Should we go to the Copper Kettle?"

Mia nodded.

"Are you both feeling okay?" said Lexi in astonishment.

"Yes, we just want cake," said Sita, an unusually determined look on her face.

"You're both cake-obsessed!" said Violet, rolling her eyes.

Willow and Bracken shared a concerned look. "Sita, maybe you shouldn't go," Willow said.

"Yes, Mia. This is getting a little odd...," Bracken began.

"We'll be back soon," Mia interrupted. "Come on, Sita." Sita didn't need any persuading.

Ignoring everyone else's puzzled looks,

they ran down the stairs and out of the house. "I don't know why, but I can't stop thinking about cake," said Sita as they jogged along the street. "It's all I can think about."

"I know. Me, too!" said Mia. They hurried up the street and turned toward the Copper Kettle.

Mia's heart sank as she saw the line of people inside, but just as they reached the door, her mom came out, holding a large cake box. "Mia!" she said. "I got here early, and I've got a cake! A big one!"

"Oh, wow!" gasped Mia. "Can we have it now?"

Her mom nodded. "Hop in the car."

"The others will wonder where we are," Mia said to Sita as they got in.

"Who cares!" said Sita, her eyes fixed on the cake box.

As soon as they got home, Mrs. Greene cut the cake, and they each had a slice. Cleo came in while they were eating. "More cake? Seriously? I'm beginning to worry about this family. What's so good about these cakes anyway?" She reached over to take the remaining slice.

"No!" Mrs. Greene grabbed the plate and pulled it away from her. "It's mine!"

Cleo blinked in shock. "Okay," she said slowly. "You can have it, Mom." She backed out of the room as Mrs. Greene started to greedily devour the last slice.

"Me full," said Alex, patting his tummy.

Mia nodded and sat back in her chair with a loud, contented sigh. Her grumpiness had melted away. All she'd needed was cake!

"Should we go upstairs?" she asked Sita. She was feeling a little guilty that they had rushed off, leaving Violet and Lexi. She pulled out her phone to text them and saw that Violet had sent a message an hour ago.

> Where are u? L and I went 2 the CK but we cdn't find u. It's really busy! We're going 2 offer 2 help. Vxx

Then there were several other messages from her.

> Mia?

> Mia? Why aren't u answering?

> Where ARE u?

"Violet left me a bunch of messages," Mia said guiltily.

"Me, too," said Sita, checking her phone.

"We'd better reply," said Mia as she started

to type.

> Hi. Sorry. We met my mom and came back 2 my house 2 have some cake. Do u want to comeover? Mxx

Violet's reply came back in just a few seconds.

> We're coming now. We think we have an idea about what's going on. Stay where u are! Vxx

Mia's fingers flew over her phone.

> Really? What? Mx

> We'll talk when we see u. Vxx

Mia put her phone down. "They're both coming here. Violet says they have an idea about what's happening."

Sita flopped onto Mia's beanbag chair. "I guess that's good, only right now, I feel so full that I just want to sleep."

"Me, too," said Mia with a yawn. "We could take a nap while we're waiting." She lay back on her bed with a sigh and the next moment was fast asleep.

Buzzzz! Buzzzz! Mia heard her phone vibrating and blinked her eyes open. She'd been deep in a dream where she had been at the Copper Kettle, eating an entire cake of her own. It tasted delicious! For a moment, she struggled to remember what day it was and what she was doing. She saw Sita curled up on the beanbag chair and remembered.

Picking up her buzzing phone, she saw Violet was calling her. She answered the call, feeling groggy. "Hi."

"Where are you?" said Violet. "We've been knocking on the door but no one's answering!"

"I'm sorry! Sita and I fell asleep. I'll come and let you in." Mia got up and shook Sita's shoulder. "Sita, the others are here."

Sita shrugged her off. "Mmm, cake," she murmured in her sleep.

Mia went downstairs, wondering why her mom hadn't let Violet and Lexi in, but as she passed her parents' bedroom, she heard her mom and Alex snoring. That was weird. Her mom never took naps during the day.

"Hi," she said, opening the door and letting Violet and Lexi in. "I'm sorry about that. We had cake, and then we all fell asleep." She saw Violet and Lexi exchange looks. "So, what's your idea?"

"Let's talk in your room," said Violet. "We can call the animals then. I think we need them with us."

As Mia turned to go upstairs, she glanced through the open kitchen door and saw the plate that the cake had been on. There were still some crumbs and scrapings of chocolate frosting on it. She felt gripped by the desire to eat them.

"Wait a sec." Going into the kitchen, she reached to scoop up the remains of the crumbs and frosting with her finger.

"No!" Violet and Lexi said together.

Violet raced over and grabbed her arm. "Don't do that."

"What? Why?" Mia said in surprise.

"Just don't," said Violet.

Mia started to feel anger build up inside her. "But I want to." Pulling her arm away from Violet, she lunged for the plate. But Violet grabbed it and lifted it out of her reach before she could get to it.

Mia felt rage fill her. She wanted cake—she needed cake! "Give it to me!" she cried angrily.

Violet dodged around the other side of the table. "No. You're not having it!"

"Why?" Mia cried.

"Don't you see, Mia?" Lexi exclaimed. "The cake from the Copper Kettle is making you act really weirdly. It must have some kind of magic in it."

"Dark magic," added Violet. "Everyone who eats those cakes is becoming obsessed with them."

Shock stopped Mia in her tracks. Magic in the cakes!

"We really need to talk," Violet said. "Let's go to your room." She put the plate down, and then she and Lexi took hold of Mia's arms and marched her upstairs.

11
Magic Recipes

The four girls and their animals sat in a circle on the floor in Mia's bedroom. Mia had Bracken on her lap, and as she petted him, she felt the longing for cake fading away slightly.

"Keep cuddling Willow," she advised Sita. "It'll help."

Sita wrapped her arms around Willow. "So, it's not someone trapping Shades to cause trouble, it's someone doing something to Mary's cakes," she said. "That's why Mia and I have been affected—we've both eaten the cakes there."

"My mom, dad, and Alex, too," said Mia.

"I thought it was strange that you kept wanting to eat more cake," Bracken said to Mia. "And that you were dreaming about it."

Looking back, Mia could see how odd it was that she had wanted cake so much.

"They are good cakes, though," sighed Sita. "That chocolate one. Mmm…."

A picture of one of Mary's chocolate cakes oozing with frosting leaped into Mia's mind, and she felt hunger start to swirl up inside her, blocking everything out. She buried her face in Bracken's fur, breathing in his sweet smell until the longing faded.

"It's such a weird feeling," she explained to the others. "It's like all you can think about is cake. It fills your thoughts. You want it so much that you feel as if you'd do anything to have it."

"You feel like you'd fight someone to get cake," Sita added. "Nothing else matters."

"What kind of magic is this?" Violet asked Sorrel.

"I suspect a charm," said Sorrel. "A spell brewed with herbs could have been put into the cake mixture."

"So, the images of the Copper Kettle that I've been seeing maybe don't have anything to do with Shades after all," said Mia. "The Star Magic could have been trying to warn me that someone was using magic in the cakes at the café."

"Mary?" said Lexi.

"Possibly, but the magic hasn't shown me her," said Mia, confused. "The only person I've seen is Mystic Maureen. Do you think the dolls and the magic cakes are linked? That Mystic Maureen is responsible for both things?"

Violet looked thoughtful. "We know she goes to the Copper Kettle. Maybe she wanted to upset Mary and snuck into the kitchen and added something to the flour or sugar."

"Or maybe it's not Mystic Maureen— maybe it's Desmond Hannigan," Lexi put in. "We know he doesn't like Mr. Jefferson, so he could have put the Shades in the dolls, and Mia and Sita both saw him in the café acting strangely."

Mia gasped. "Maybe he and Mystic Maureen are in this together!"

"They could be working as a team!" exclaimed Bracken.

Juniper jumped around, chattering excitedly. "Yes! Yes!"

"Wait!" said Sita. "It doesn't make sense. Why would Mystic Maureen or Desmond Hannigan want to make people desperate to eat Mary's cakes?"

"I can see that Desmond Hannigan might want the cakes to taste horrible so no one would go to the Copper Kettle, but why would he want to make them taste so good that people can't stop eating them? You're right—it doesn't make sense," Violet reasoned.

"The spell doesn't just make people want to eat cake, though," said Mia, thinking of her family. "It's making people really angry. Maybe that's why he was doing it."

"But it's meant business is booming for Mary, and his café is losing customers," said Violet.

"It's all so confusing!" said Lexi in frustration. "Are the Shades and the cakes linked?"

"Mia, why don't you use magic and see if it shows you anything that can help us figure this out," suggested Willow.

Mia pulled her mirror out of her pocket and drew on the magic current. "Show me anything that can help," she told it, and an image appeared.

"I can see the Copper Kettle," she told the others. "It's filled with people. Ooh." She blinked as she took in the whole scene. "Two people are fighting over a cake, and there's a lot of arguing. Mary looks really worried."

The image changed.

"It's showing me something else," Mia said. "It's that picture I've seen before of Mystic Maureen in front of a mirror with lights all around it." Mia saw something she hadn't noticed before. On the dressing table, there was an old brown book. It looked just like Mary's grandma's journal….

She frowned. Why did Mystic Maureen have Mary's grandma's journal? She noticed that there was some faded gold writing on the cover.

"Show me the journal in the picture," she told the magic.

"What journal?" asked Violet, who couldn't see anything.

Mia waved for her to be quiet as the magic zoomed in on the journal so she could read the words on the cover: *Magic Recipes.*

"Magic!" she gasped, looking up at the others. "Mary's recipe book from her grandma has magic recipes in it!"

The animals leaped to their feet, and the girls started talking all at once.

"That journal's not just a book of baking, it's a book of magic!" Sita gasped.

"No wonder she was worried that someone might try to steal it," said Mia. "Mary always says there's a bit of magic in the ice cream. I thought she was joking, but she must have been telling the truth!"

"A bit of magic in the ice cream and a lot in the cakes," said Violet. "Mary must be making magic cakes! But why would she want to make people angry?"

"And what do the cakes have to do with the dolls and the Shades?" said Lexi. "Mary is really good friends with the Jeffersons—she wouldn't want to upset them. And the magic showed Mystic Maureen with the book, not Mary. Are we looking for two people doing dark magic or one?"

Violet got to her feet. "We need to talk

to Mary."

"Sita, you might have to use your powers," said Sorrel. "If she is doing dark magic, then you must be ready to command her to obey you."

Sita nodded confidently. "Okay. I'll be ready."

For a moment, Mia remembered how nervous Sita used to be about doing magic when she had first discovered her abilities. Using magic and being Star Friends had changed them all since last autumn.

Violet pointed to the shadows beside Mia's wardrobe. "I vote we take the quickest way to the Copper Kettle!" she said.

Bracken licked Mia's hand. "Good luck!"

Violet was waiting in the shadows. Mia, Lexi, and Sita stepped forward, held hands, and then the shadows closed around them, the magic whisking them away.

12
Chaos at the Copper Kettle

The shadows cleared, and Mia saw that Violet had transported them to the woods just across the main street from the Copper Kettle. "I didn't dare risk us appearing inside," said Violet.

"It doesn't look like there'd be room anyway!" Mia exclaimed.

Through the windows, she could see people filling every bit of space. They were elbowing each other out of the way as they tried to get to the counter to buy cakes. Raised, angry voices floated across the street to the girls.

"This doesn't look good," said Sita.

"Come on—let's see if we can help. If we can get rid of everyone, then maybe we can talk to Mary alone," said Mia.

She led the way across the street, and they pushed their way inside. People were crowded around the counter, yelling at Mary, who was close to tears.

"I want to buy cake!"

"Sell us cake!"

Their faces were red and angry. Mia spotted Mr. Jefferson's tall, thin figure at the front, banging his fists on the counter. A memory stirred. Had he been the man who broke in? She would never have thought it possible, but right now, he looked angry enough to do anything.

Mia motioned to the others, and they edged their way closer to the counter.

"Go away! Please!" Mary pleaded. If she were the one doing dark magic, it didn't look as if it were making her happy.

"No!" yelled an older man. "I want cake!" Mia realized it was her next-door neighbor, friendly Mr. Jones.

A woman picked up a salt shaker. It was Mia's teacher, Miss Harris. "Give us cake!" she screamed. She threw the shaker at the wall behind Mary. It hit one of the old Victorian dolls on the shelf. The doll fell to the ground.

"Be careful!" gasped Mary.

Mia ducked underneath the partition, and the others followed.

"Girls, what are you doing here?" Mary turned panicked eyes on them. "You could get hurt."

"Grandma!" exclaimed Sita in horror as she spotted her grandma in the crowd.

But her grandma didn't even seem to notice her. Her eyes were glazed over as though she were possessed. She picked up a sugar bowl and hurled it at the wall.

"CAKE!" everyone shouted, starting to throw anything they could get their hands on—plates, saucers, spoons….

"Quick, let's get out of here!" cried Violet, ducking as a plate smashed against the wall above her head. She ran to the door that led upstairs to Mary's apartment and pulled it open. "Mary! Come on!"

The customers started climbing over the

counter. Mia pushed her friends through the door and slammed it shut behind them. Luckily, there was a key in the lock. She turned it quickly and was only just in time. The people on the other side started pounding on the door, banging and yelling. Mia's scalp prickled as she realized it was the door she had seen in her dream.

"CAKE! CAKE! CAKE!" they shouted.

Mary rushed up the stairs to her apartment, and the girls followed. "Oh, what am I going to do?" she cried. "They've all gone crazy."

"Or, they've eaten cake with a magic charm inside it…," said Violet pointedly.

Mary's face paled. "How do you know?"

Mia spotted the journal on the coffee table. "Magic recipes," she said, picking it up. "You've been using magic, haven't you, Mary?"

Mary started to shake her head. "No … no…."

"Enough!" Sita cut in. Her voice sounded stern, completely unlike her usual soft tone, and Mia realized she was using her powers. Mary fell silent. "People are going to get hurt, Mary, if this continues," Sita continued. "We have to stop it. We can help you, but you must tell us the truth. Have you been using magic?"

Mary nodded. "I have. I didn't mean for it to end up like this. I just wanted people to want to eat my cakes." She picked up the journal. "My grandma was fascinated by magic and used charms made from plants to help people with illnesses and to make her food taste good. When she died, she left me her book with all of her magical notes in it. I've only ever used it to add just a little magic charm to my ice cream, but when all of my customers started going to the marina, I thought I'd use it to make cakes that people couldn't resist."

"It certainly worked!" said Violet.

"I didn't realize this would happen," Mary said anxiously. "I just wanted more customers. It's all gotten completely out of control. I can't believe the magic is so powerful that people are smashing plates, breaking in…."

Someone on the other side of the door now seemed to be using something large to try to break it down.

"What am I going to do?" Mary said fearfully.

"Don't worry," Sita said. "We're going to figure this out, and while we're doing that, you're going to go to your room and take a little nap. You will go to sleep until I wake you. Do you understand?"

Mary nodded, stood up, and moved like a sleepwalker to her bedroom.

"Great job, Sita," Mia said. "Now what?"

"Now we figure this chaos out," said Sita grimly.

The girls hurried to the staircase that led down to the door into the café. The banging and yelling were getting even louder. "How are we going to get rid of everyone?" shouted Lexi above the noise.

"Let's call the animals and see if they have any ideas," said Mia.

The animals appeared and listened while the girls told them what was going on.

"You can't open that door," said Sorrel in alarm. "All of those people will come charging in here, and they sound really angry. There's no telling what they'll do."

"But we have to get Sita into the café so she can command them to go home," said Mia.

"We need a distraction so Sita can get through the door and into the café," said Willow.

Juniper leaped onto the windowsill. "I know! I can get through the landing window and into the café, and Lexi can climb down after me, using her agility! I bet between us we can get everyone away from the door!"

"Good plan, Juniper!" In a flash, Lexi was by the window. She opened it, and Juniper leaped out. Lexi grinned at the others. "See you in a bit!" She followed Juniper out of the window.

The others raced to the bottom of the stairs. A minute later, they heard the angry shouts turning to cries of surprise. "There's a squirrel in here!"

"What's it doing? It's leaping around everywhere!"

There was a scream. "It's on my head! Get it off me!"

"Cake!" they heard Lexi shout. "Hey, everyone, there's cake over here!"

"Cake? Where?"

"Where's the cake?"

The banging on the door stopped. Mia saw her chance and pushed the door open. Everyone was either looking at Lexi or at Juniper. As well as Mr. Jefferson, Miss Harris, Mr. Jones, and Sita's grandma, she could see Alyssa, Hannah, and Sadie—girls from their class.

"Go!" she hissed to the animals.

They leaped into the café, making people shout and stagger, forgetting about cake in their surprise and confusion. "A fox!"

"A deer and a cat!"

"What's going on?"

"Now, Sita!" exclaimed Mia, pulling a chair over to the counter.

"QUIET!" Sita commanded, climbing up onto the counter. "No one must speak or move again until I command it."

The whole room fell still. Mia tried to open her mouth and found that she couldn't speak, either. The animals were also frozen to the spot. "Mia, Violet, Lexi, and the animals, you can all move and speak," Sita said hastily, realizing what she'd done. Mia felt a rush of relief as her body and voice came under her control again. Sita's magic was really powerful, and scary!

Sita cleared her throat. "Everyone except for Violet, Lexi, Mia, and the animals—you are all to go home. You do not want to eat cake anymore. When you walk out of the door, you will forget about everything that has happened in here. You will go home and feel relaxed and happy, thinking about what a nice time you've had at the Copper Kettle and wanting to come back again soon."

Mia was impressed. Sita had become very good at giving magic commands.

"Now go!" Sita instructed. Suddenly, everyone started moving again. The girls watched as people dazedly rubbed their heads and wandered out onto the street, their anger and desire for cake completely forgotten. Sita's grandmother hesitated, looking at her. "Go home, Grandma," Sita said forcefully, and her grandma nodded and left.

As the last person went out, Willow butted the door shut. Lexi joined her, locked the door, and turned the sign that said *Open* to *Closed*. "Phew!" she exclaimed.

Violet looked at the doorway that led upstairs. "Time to go and talk to Mary," she said.

They went upstairs to the apartment. Mary's bedroom door was open, and they could see that she was still asleep, lying on top of the covers, breathing peacefully. As they walked in, Mia stopped in her tracks. Mary's dressing table was opposite the bed. It had a mirror surrounded by lights, exactly the same as the one that she had seen Mystic Maureen sitting at. But why would Mystic Maureen have been in Mary's bedroom, unless … unless….

Her eyes caught sight of the multicolored scarf hanging over the back of the chair, and on top of it was a beaded necklace with a large M hanging from it.

It was as if a light bulb had gone off in Mia's head. Suddenly, she realized why the image of Mystic Maureen sitting at the mirror had always nagged at her. The reflection in the mirror had shown Mystic Maureen with her shoulder-length red hair, but from the back, the figure had short brown hair and had looked just like…

"Mary!" she exclaimed. "Mary is Mystic Maureen!"

13
BEST FRIENDS – AND MAGIC – FOREVER

Everyone stared at Mia.

"What do you mean?" demanded Lexi.

"Have you solved the mystery, Mia?" Bracken asked, bouncing around in delight.

"I think so. Look!" Mia grabbed the necklace with the M pendant from the chair and the scarf. "Mystic Maureen was wearing this necklace and this scarf. Mary must have disguised herself as her with magic."

"Using a glamour!" Violet exclaimed. She smacked her forehead. "Of course!

Why didn't I think of that?"

"It all makes sense now. It's why the Copper Kettle kept appearing in my visions! I even knew that Mary collected dolls, just like Mystic Maureen said she did," Mia said, glancing at the dolls on the shelf and thinking of the others downstairs. "I just didn't put it all together!"

"No wonder we haven't been able to find where Mystic Maureen lives or works," said Lexi. "She never really existed. She was Mary in disguise!"

"But why?" Sita said. "I thought she liked the Jeffersons."

"I think you need to wake her up and ask her about it," Sorrel said.

"Hide," Violet urged the animals. "Sita can make her forget you, but if she sees you, she's bound to ask questions, and we want to find out what's been going on as quickly as possible."

The animals vanished.

"Do your stuff, Sita," said Mia. The others nodded.

"Mary," said Sita, going over to the bed. "I want you to wake up now."

Mary stirred, mumbling a little in her sleep. Rubbing her eyes, she sat up. "What's happening?" she said dazedly, and then her eyes widened as she remembered. "The café! The people!"

"It's all right," said Sita soothingly. "They're all gone. There's nothing for you to worry about now. Just some cleaning up to do."

Mary relaxed. "Oh, thank goodness." She looked at Sita anxiously. "You won't tell anyone I put a charm in the cakes, will you?"

"No," said Sita. "But you can't do it anymore."

Mary nodded. "I won't. I wanted business to pick up, but I shouldn't have used magic the way I did. It isn't the answer." She rubbed her forehead. "It can be so hard to control."

"Mary, have you used magic before? Did you use it to disguise yourself as Mystic Maureen? And to conjure Shades?" Sita asked.

Even though Mia knew the answer, it was still a shock when Mary nodded.

"But why?" Lexi burst out.

"I just wanted to help," Mary said unhappily.

"Help?" echoed Violet. "But how could conjuring Shades help? They're evil."

"I didn't realize that," Mary said. "There were notes in the back of the journal about all kinds of different magic—using glamours, conjuring Shades. It didn't say Shades were evil, and I just thought if I conjured Heart's Desire Shades, they would make Mike's wish to win the Prettiest Small Town competition come true, and if that happened, the Copper Kettle would get busier. I didn't know that they would do all of those awful things. I wanted to stop them, but I didn't know how. Thankfully, one day they just vanished."

The girls exchanged looks. The Shades had only stopped when Violet had sent them back to the shadows, but Mary didn't need to know that.

"So, how did you do it?" Sita asked. "How did you trap the Shades in Mrs. Jefferson's dolls?"

"I went to their house disguised as Mystic Maureen, and when I was there, I used my phone."

"Your phone?" repeated Mia. "How?"

"My grandma had written that a Shade can be trapped if you capture its likeness. I conjured them with my grandma's magic spell and then trapped them by taking pictures with my phone."

Suddenly, another of the clues Mia had seen made sense—the rectangular black object was Mary's cell phone, not a remote control!

"Then what did you do?" Sita asked.

"I went to Ana's and transferred the Shades from my phone to the dolls. I wish I'd never done it." Her eyes filled with tears. "I feel so guilty."

Mia didn't know what to do. They'd never had to deal with someone who'd been using dark magic to try to do good before.

Sita took Mary's hand. "It's all right, Mary. You're going to get up, and then we're all going to go downstairs and help clean up," she instructed. "You're going to forget that we know about magic. You're going to feel relieved that the magic cake is all gone, and you're going to decide that you will never use your grandma's magic book ever again, except for adding a little magic to the ice cream. Do you understand?"

"I understand," said Mary, her eyes on Sita's.

"Then let's go and clean up," said Sita, helping Mary off the bed.

They went downstairs and began clearing away the broken china and cleaning the tables. They carefully swept up any remaining crumbs of cake. Mia's tummy rumbled at the sight of them. She longed to grab them and eat them, but she fought the urge. *No cake,* she told herself firmly. *The cake is bad.* Lexi saw her face and quickly put the crumbs in the garbage can.

They were almost finished when there was a knock on the door.

"It's Desmond Hannigan," Mia said in surprise. They'd been wrong about him being involved, but why was he here now?

Mary went to the door and unlocked it. "I'm afraid we're closed at the moment."

"I don't want to have a cup of tea or buy

a cake," he said brusquely. "I'm here with a business proposition for you. Can I come in?"

Mary opened the door, and he walked in.

"It's come to my attention that the ice cream you sell here is far superior to the ice cream that's on sale at the marina café," he said, clearing his throat. "I want to know whether you would be interested in supplying your ice cream to the Friendly Fish from now on."

"That's a great idea," Mia said in delight. "You'll make a lot of money, Mary, and then it won't matter if the Copper Kettle is a little quiet."

But to her surprise, Mary looked worried. "I don't know. I've never supplied another business before."

"It'd be great!" said Violet. "Selling your ice cream at the marina would mean a lot more people could enjoy it."

"I'd have to hire more staff and buy more equipment," Mary fretted. "It would be very different."

"Maybe," said Sita. "But that doesn't mean it'd be bad. When things change, life often gets even better." She gave Mia a quick smile. "I realized that yesterday."

Mary nodded slowly. "I guess so. After all, it was a big change when I started the Copper Kettle, and that worked out for the best."

Desmond Hannigan cleared his throat. "So, do you want to go into business with me?" he asked.

The girls looked hopefully at Mary.

"Yes," she said, smiling. "I do."

After the café was cleaned up and Mary was
happily settled back upstairs, figuring out how
she could make enough ice cream for two
businesses, the girls ran to the clearing.

"Bracken!"

"Sorrel!"

"Juniper!"

"Willow!"

The animals appeared, questions tumbling
out of them.

"What happened?" said Bracken.

"Did you figure everything out?" asked
Willow.

"What happened to the cake?" demanded
Juniper.

"Did you stop that woman from doing
magic?" Sorrel said sharply.

"Yes, it's all fixed," said Mia happily.

"Mary never meant to hurt anyone," Violet

said, crouching down and petting Sorrel.
"She only wanted to help Mr. Jefferson
and her business. She didn't realize she was
doing such powerful magic. It just got out of
control."

"She's never going to use that magic journal
again," Sita told Willow.

"And all of the magic cake has been thrown
away," Lexi said, cuddling Juniper.

"She's also agreed to make ice cream for the
marina," said Mia. "Which means the Copper
Kettle will stay open even if there aren't quite
as many customers."

"That'll probably be good for Mary," said
Sita. "I don't think she liked being so busy!"

"Everything worked out perfectly," Mia
declared. "There's nothing to worry about
anymore." She glanced at Sita. "Is there?"

Sita smiled. "No. If I can stop an angry mob
of bewitched people, I think I'll be able to
cope with the state tests. I'm not even going

to worry about starting middle school. It'll be a big change, but it'll be fine. We're all going to stay best friends, continuing to fight dark magic and making people happy, and that's all that really matters."

Willow rubbed her head against her. "I've been telling you that for weeks."

Sita kissed her. "I know. I should have listened to you."

"Don't forget that we still have one more quarter at Westport to go before we leave," said Lexi. "Okay, I doubt Mom will let me out of the house while we're doing state tests, but after that, we have the school trip! It's kind of scary, but I bet it'll be fun."

"We also have sports day and the fifth-grade play to look forward to," put in Mia.

"And the end-of-year math challenge!" said Violet, beaming.

"Yay!" said Lexi excitedly.

Mia and Sita shook their heads at each other

and grinned.

Mia held up her hand for a high five. "Whatever happens, we all know that magic is forever!"

The others met her hand with theirs. "Forever!" they echoed, and then they all spun away, laughing.

Lexi chased after Juniper, while Willow cantered away with Sita in pursuit. Sorrel pressed against Violet's legs, purring loudly.

Mia crouched down, and Bracken put a paw on her knee. Happiness rushed through her as she gathered him in her arms and he licked her nose.

"Things may change this year, but we're going to love each other forever, aren't we, Bracken?" she whispered. "Whatever happens, wherever I go, you'll always be with me, won't you?"

"Always," he promised, his soft fur tickling her face and his eyes shining star-bright.